Princess Maent

and

the Boy

on

the Beach

Princess Maent

and

the Boy on the Beach

a story to read and ten things you can make

GERALD ROBINSON

wrote the words and drew the pictures

RESOURCE *Publications* · Eugene, Oregon

PRINCESS MAENT AND THE BOY ON THE BEACH
a story to read and ten things you can make

Resource Publications
An Imprint of Wipf and Stock Publishers
199 W. 8th Ave., Suite 3,
Eugene, OR 97401

www.wipfandstock.com

PAPERBACK ISBN: 978-1-7252-8077-9

HARDCOVER ISBN: 978-1-7252-8076-2

EBOOK ISBN: 978-1-7252-8078-6

Manufactured in the U.S.A.

Ten Things You Can Make

this book belongs to

PRINCESS MAENT

and the BOY on the BEACH

My name is
Princess Maent.

I live in a castle.
My castle is
the Castle Perigord,
and I have a cat.

My cat's name
is Samantha
but I call her Sammi
for short.

She lives with me
in my castle.

I sit in a big big chair. It is called a throne,
and I wear a crown because I am a Princess.

Sammi sits on a tiny chair.
Her chair is called a footstool.

She wears a tiny crown
because she is a princess's cat.

Sammi and I live at the very top of my castle.
My castle is at the top of a vey high hill.
There is a road to the castle
　　but the hill is so steep
　　　　the road can't go straight up.
The road has to go round-and-round,
　　　and round-and-round,
　　　　　and round-and-round,
　　　to get to the top.
So to get to my castle you have to go
round-and-round,
　　　and round-and-round,
　　　　　and round-and-round.
My room is at the very top of the castle.
Through my window I can see a long way
I can see right across the fields
　　to a sandy beach.
The beach is yellow, and beyond it is the sea.

The sea is green, and over it the sky is blue.
The sky is blue with white clouds.
The clouds are blowing in the wind.
The winds are blowing and blowing.
They are blowing a sailboat with a white sail.
       I have a telescope in my room.
It lets me see things that are far far away.
I look at the beach through my telescope
    and I see a boy playing with his dog.
I have no one to play with.
I would like the boy to play with me,
but how can I do that?

The boy's name is Peter
The dog's name is Roger
Peter has a ball
The ball is red
The dog is black.
Peter throws the ball.

Roger runs and runs after it. He brings the ball
back to Peter. Peter throws the ball again.
Roger chases after it again.
He brings the ball back to Peter again.
Peter throws the ball into the sea.

The sea is green, the ball is red.
The red ball floats on the green sea.
Roger chases after it.
He makes lots of white splashes,
white splashes on his black fur.
He grabs the ball in his mouth
and brings it back to Peter.
Peter and Roger are having fun.

Princess Maent says "I'd like to have fun too.
I will write a letter to Peter and Roger.
I will get some paper and a pen and write a letter
to Peter and Roger."

She writes "Dear Peter (and Roger),
My name is Princess Maent,
I live at the very top of the Castle Perigord.
I would like you to come and play with me.
Come and have tea."
Then she folds the paper
to make a paper airplane:

(Tomorrow you can make a plane like that.)

1. To make a Paper Airplane
(it's not hard) Take a sheet of paper, and

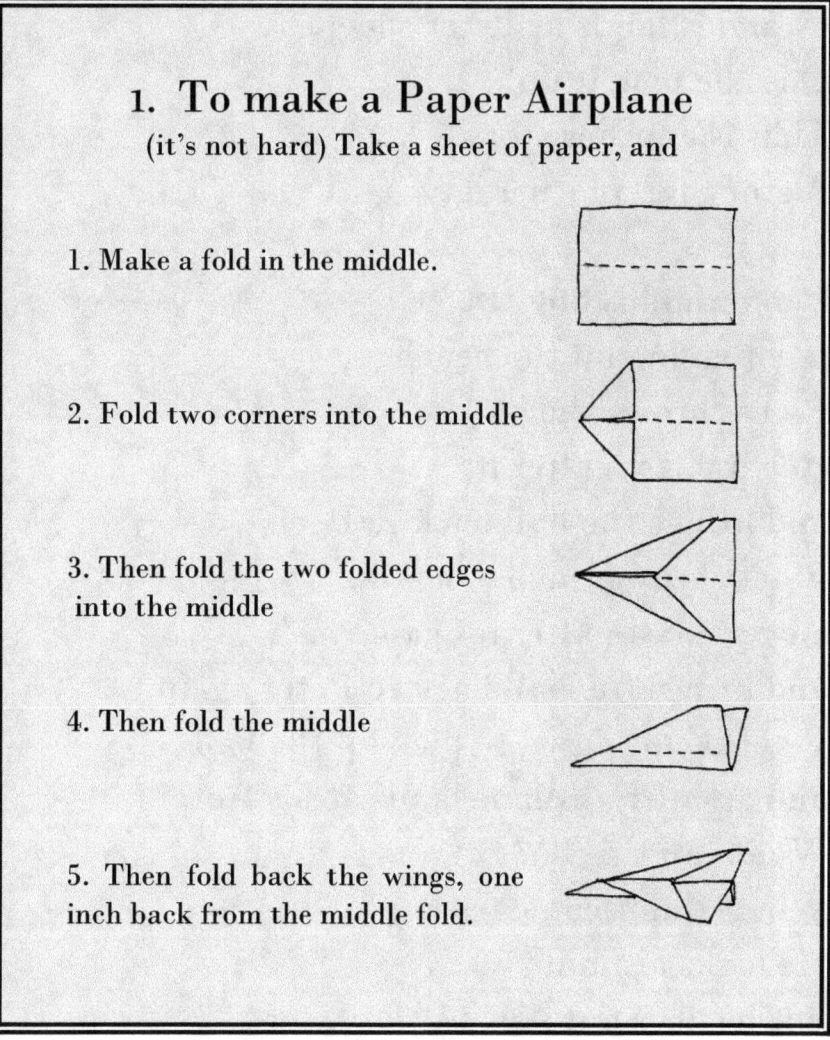

1. Make a fold in the middle.

2. Fold two corners into the middle

3. Then fold the two folded edges into the middle

4. Then fold the middle

5. Then fold back the wings, one inch back from the middle fold.

She throws the airplane out the window.
The winds blow it this way.
The winds blow it that way.
The winds blow it this way and that way,

and it lands at Peter's feet.
Does he pick it up?
That is another story.
A story for another day.

Peter and his dog Roger
are playing on the beach.
Peter throws the ball.
Roger chases after it
and brings the ball back to Peter.
Peter throws the ball again.
Roger chases after it again
and brings the ball back to Peter again.
Peter bends down to pick up the ball
and a paper airplane lands at his feet.
What can this be?
Where did it come from?
He looks around
but he does not see anybody.
He calls out
"Who's there?"
but nobody answers.
Nobody except Roger.
Roger says "Rowf!"

He unfolds the paper airplane
and sees there is a message.
The message says:
"Dear Peter (and Roger)
My name is Princess Maent,
I live at the very top of the Castle Perigord.
I would like you to come and play with me.
Come and have tea."
Peter says to Roger
"Come along Roger,
We are going to have tea.
We'll play with the princess,
then we'll have tea."
        Roger says "Rowf!"
They walk across the green fields.
They walk up to the hill with the castle.
The hill is too steep for them to climb
so they take the road that goes round-and-round,
        and round-and-round,
                and round-and-round the hill.
They follow the road
and go round-and-round,
        and round-and-round,
                and round-and-round, until

they arrive at the door of the castle.
The castle door is very big.
It has a big knocker.
Peter reaches up for it.
He reaches way way up,
and knocks at the door.
A voice from inside says
"Halt! I am the Inner Guard.
Who comes here?"

"We are Peter and Roger. We have come
to play with the Princess, and have tea."
The Inner Guard says
"Halt, while I make due report."
The Inner Guard calls the Royal Equerry
"Honored Sir, outside the door of the castle
stand Peter and Roger,
a boy and his dog,
to play with the Princess
and have tea."
The Royal Equerry asks
"How do they hope to obtain those privileges?"
"By the invitation of the Princess."
"The invitation of the Princess
has already been extended in their favor,

so you will admit them in due form
but let them take heed
upon what they enter."
A tiny door hidden in the big door opens
and Peter and Roger go through it.
The Royal Equerry leads the way.
They go up stairs,
        and up stairs,
                and up stairs,
        to the room of the Princess.
She is sitting on her throne.
Next to her is Sammi.
Sammi is sitting on her footstool.
The Royal Equerry announces
"Master Peter and Master Roger!"
The Princess stands up and says
"Thank you for coming to play with me."
They put their party hats on.
(Tomorrow you can make a party hat)
They play Chase the Ball,
        and Blind Man's Buff,
                and Hide and Seek.
They are having a lot of fun.
Then the Princess rings a little bell

2. To make a Party Hat
(like the Princess's Crown)
You will need some sheets of paper, scissors, and a glue stick.

1.Fold a sheet of paper in three, lengthways.

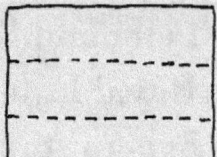

2. Cut V-shaped notches in one edge, then cut along the fold lines.

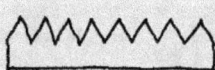

3. Glue sections end-to-end to make a band.

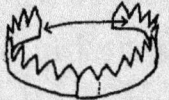

For a child's party hat you will need to glue two sections together. For an adult you will need two-and-a-half sections, and for a cat one section should do.

and their tea arrives. They have carrot sticks,
and peanut butter sandwiches made with jam,
and pieces of left-over birthday cake,
and dog food for Roger,
and cat food for Sammi.

Suddenly they hear a loud noise.

"Bang!
　　　Bang Bang!
　　　　Bang Bang Bang!
The Inner Guard says "Sir, there is an alarm!"
The Royal Equerry says
"Ascertain the cause of that alarm."
The Inner Guard shouts
"Halt! Who comes here?"
"I am the Red King.
I have come
to marry the Princess
and live in the castle."
The Inner Guard says
"Halt, while I make due report."
The Inner Guard calls the Royal Equerry
"Honored Sir, outside the door of the castle
stands the Red King
who wishes to live in this castle."
"How does he hope to obtain that privilege?"
"By marrying the Princess."
"His request to marry the Princess
has already been deemed unacceptable.
(that means the Princess said "No")
so tell him he will have to go."

The Inner Guard calls out to the Red King
"Sir, your application to the Princess
has already been deemed unacceptable
so you may not enter here."
The Red King is angry. He replies
"Then I will come back with my Red Army.
We will break down the door
and make the Princess our prisoner
and take over the castle!"
and he goes off
in a huff.
The Inner Guard tells the Royal Equerry
what the Red King has said.
The Royal Equerry tells the Princess.
The Princess tells Peter, saying
"Oh dear! Oh dear! Oh dear!"
Whatever shall we do?
I do not want to marry him,
I'd rather marry you!"
"We must escape" says Peter.
"We must fly away.
"We will make ourselves a kite
and leave this very day."
Quickly, quickly they make a kite

(Tomorrow you can make a kite like that)

3. To make a Kite

You will need

1. Two sticks or canes about as thick as a pencil; one about 36 inches long, and the other 30 inches.
2. A roll of wrapping paper, about 30 inches wide.
3. Eight strips of cloth, about 2 inches by 10 inches
4. Pencil, scissors, white glue, and
5. A ball of string.

Here's what to do . . .

1. Lay the shorter stick across the longer one, about 15 inches from one end, and tie them together, running the string criss-cross. Put some glue on the knot.

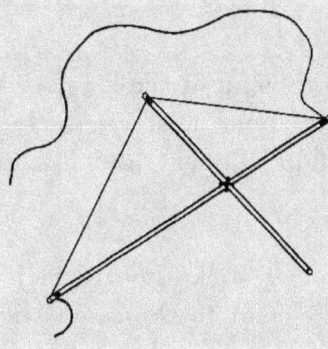

2. Tie a piece of string to the bottom of the long stick and pull it very tight, putting some glue on the knot. Then tie the string to the end of the next stick, and so on, until you end up where you started.
3. Lay the cross on a piece of wrapping paper. Draw a line on the paper all round the strings. Trim off the paper 2 inches outside that line.

(continued on next page)

(continued from previous page)

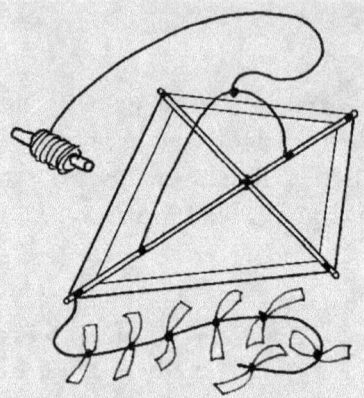

4. Put the cross back on the paper, and fold the edges of the paper over the strings, and glue them down, and your kite is made.

To make the tail:

Tie an 8-foot piece of string to the end of the long stick. Make a slip-knot in the string, poke a strip of cloth through the loop, and pull tight. Repeat about eight times.

To rig the kite:

Tie a piece of string to the longer stick about 6 inches from the top, and tie the other end to the same stick about 9 inches from the bottom, leaving a loop of about 12 inches. Make a slip-knot near the middle of the loop and tie the end of your ball of string to it.

To fly the kite: wait for a day when there is some wind. Tie the end of the ball of string to the loop of string on the kite. If the kite flies flat or does not rise move the string down the loop. If it darts around or is unstable move the string up the loop.

Have fun!

The kite has a long tail.
They carry the kite up to the castle roof.
Peter holds on to the end of the kite.
The Princess holds on to Peter.
Roger holds on to the tail of the kite.
Sammi holds on to Roger's tail,
and they wait for the wind.
The wind starts to blow: Woo and whoosh,
    Whoosh and woo,
       Woo and whoosh.
It blows the kite right off the roof.
It blows the kite up into the sky,
away from the castle, so high, so high.
And then a hill comes into view,
a hill with three trees on its top.
The trees are Oak and Ash and Yew,

and this is where they gently drop.

The Oak Tree says
"I am here because I am strong.
I can stand here all year long.
When winter storms rage helter-skelter
I'm the one to give them shelter,
—and my leaves are curly."

The Ash Tree says
"I am here because I am loved
by sparrows, finches, robins, doves.
I am the tree the birds love best
so I am where they build their nests
—and my leaves are shiny."

The Yew Tree says
"I am here because I am old.
I have watched the world unfold.
I was old when the world was new
and soon I will remember you,
—and my leaves are needles."

Sammi asked the trees "Why do you grow at the top of a hill?"

"We grow at the top of a hill" said the Oak
". . . because we are friends" said the Ash.

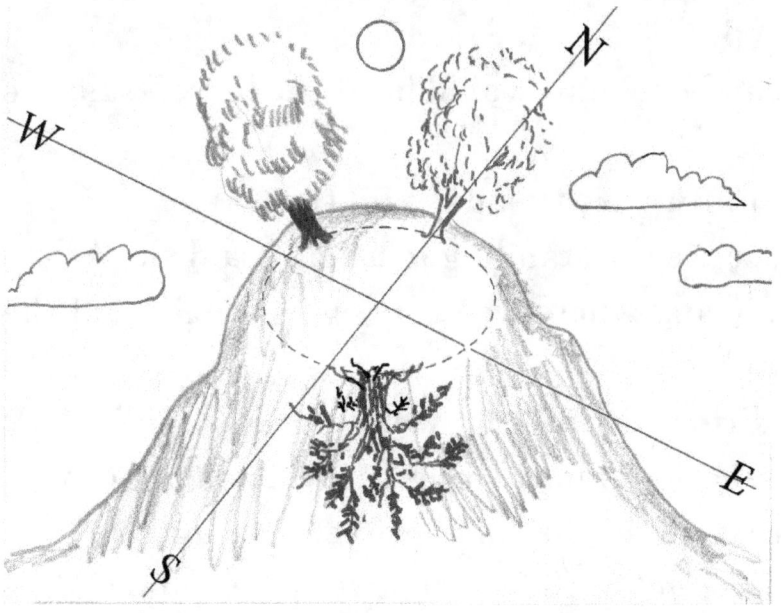

"If we were on the side of the hill" said the Yew
". . . one of us would be the highest" said the Oak,
". . . and one of us would be in the middle" said
the Ash,
". . . and one of us would be lowest." said the
Yew.
Then Sammi asked "And why do you grow in a
ring?"
"We grow in a ring" said the Oak
". . . because we are friends" said the Ash.
"If we grew in a straight line" said the Yew

". . . one of us would be at the front" said the Oak,
". . . and one of us would be in the middle" said
the Ash,
". . . and one of us would be at the back," said the
Yew,
". . . but we are friends" said the Oak,
". . . so we are standing in a ring" said the Ash,
". . . a ring where we share everything" said the
Yew.
The Princess said "We will be friends too!"
 and she stood in the ring between Oak and Ash.
Peter stood in the ring between Ash and Yew,
Roger stood in the ring between Yew and Oak,
And Sammi sat down in the middle
    because Sammi is the Princess's cat.
As friends they had no secrets
so they told the trees about the Red King.
How he had knocked at the door and said
"I will come back with my Red Army.
We will break down the door
and make the Princess our prisoner
and take over the castle."
The Oak Tree said:
"We heard another story.

We heard the Red King went south.
He visited the Black King
to ask him to send his Black Army
to help him capture the castle."
The Ash Tree said:
"We heard the Red King went north.
He visited the White King
to ask him to send his White Army
to help him capture the castle."
The Yew Tree said:
"The three kings have a castle each
but none among them has a beach
from which they'd launch a ship abroad.
That's why they want your Perigord."
The Princess said "Oh dear! Oh dear!
Whatever shall we do?
The Red Army was bad enough
without the other two."
Peter said "We have a need
to put our thinking caps on
then we'll know
what to do."
(Tomorrow you can make a thinking cap.)
 They put their thinking caps on

19

and then they saw the light. . .
"We'll need an army of our own
 if we are going to fight."

4. To make a Thinking Cap

You will need:

1. Two sheets of paper,
2. A piece of string 36 inches long,
3. Pencil, scissors, a ruler, and a glue stick.

Here's what to do . . .

1. Lay one of the sheets across the other and trim off what overhangs to make the sheets square.

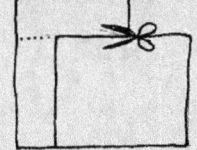

2. Fold a corner into the middle and tuck the string behind it. Mark a glue line by drawing a line one inch from a side corner to the top corner.

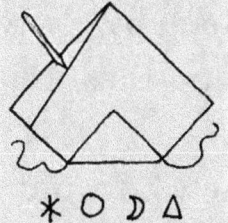

3. Decorate your cap by drawing some mystical signs on it.

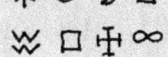

4. Spread glue on the glue area and, bending the paper away from you, join the two long edges. The strings are to tie under your chin.

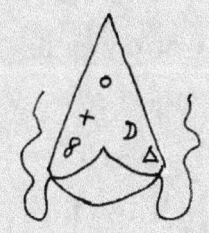

"But where could we get an army?" Sammi asks.
"You can't go east" the Oak Tree said
"Because that is where the Red Army is."

21

"You can't go south" the Ash Tree said
"Because that is where the Black Army is."
"You can't go north" the Yew Tree said
"Because that is where the White Army is."
"That settles it" said Peter,
"We'll all go west."
A west wind blows across he sky.
They grab the kite and start to fly.
OAK and ASH and YEW all say
"HE'S AWAY!!" and then "OK!!"
"Good bye" say Oak and Ash and Yew
"Fare-thee-well and Toodle-loo."

The west wind whisks them to the coast.
The West Coast's where it rains the most.
The West Coast's known for being wet.
Vancouver is the wettest yet.
 "I need a new hat" Sammi said.
"This rain is raining on my head!"
So while the rain around them splats
They make themselves some paper hats.

5. To make a Paper Hat

Take a page from a newspaper, and

1. Half way down the page. fold it in half.

2. Fold a top corner into the middle

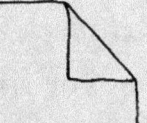

3. Do the same with the other top corner so they meet in the middle.

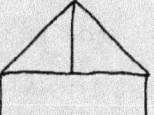

4. Fold up a 1½ inch strip of the bottom of the upper sheet

5.Repeat this until you reach the folded top corners.

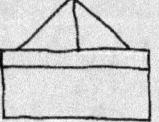

6. Turn the hat over and repeat 4 and 5 for the other bottom edge strip. You can now wear your paper hat.

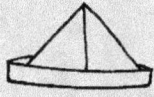

(Tomorrow you can
make a hat
just like the one
that hides the cat.
You are good at
origamis,
so you can make one
just like Sammi's.)

The Princess said "Oh dear. Oh dear.
We'll never find an army here.
An army here would sink in mud.
I think our project here's a dud.
It's just too wet to have an army.
Looking for one here is barmy.
Let's go eastwards where it's dry."
(An east wind lifts them to the sky.)

They land in Addis Ababa.
That's in Ethi-
Opi-
Ah.
Ethiopia's Dry & Hot.
"Yes . . . but it's a dry heat!"
It's a dry heat, true, but dry or not,

6. To make a Paper Fan

You will need:
1. A sheet of paper,
2. A six-inch piece of string,
3. Scotch tape, scissors and a spring-type paper clip. Here's what to do:

1. Make a fold half-an-inch from the short edge of a piece of paper. Turn the sheet over and make another fold half-an- inch from the first fold. Continue the process until the whole sheet is folded into a zig-zag. Squeeze the folds together, and clamp with a paper clip.

2. Tie a knot to make a loop of your piece of string. Make a one-inch cut along one of the fold lines near the middle of the bunch, and slide the middle of your string loop into the cut.

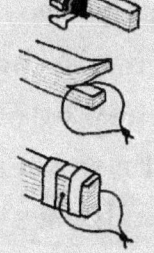

3. Squeeze the ends of the zig-zags together, and wrap a piece of Scotch tape around them. Pull the loop up to the tape, then wrap a piece of tape round folds on other side of the loop

4. Remove the paper clip and spread out your fan. Cool!

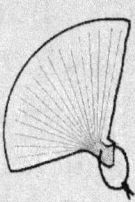

Sammi says
"It's still too hot!
A fan would make
     a cooling breeze
Could someone get one
     for me, please?"
(tomorrow you can make a one
just like Sammi's paper fan.)

The army there is fast asleep
     even though it's day.
They say "It's just too hot to fight.
     Now please just go away!"
The Princess says "Let's fly up north.
It's not so hot up there."
So they hitch a ride on a north wind
And rise up in the air.
They fly way up to Moscow
where it's really really cold.
"Yes . . . but it's a dry cold!"
(that's what we were told)
but Sammi said
(and shook her head)
"It's still too cold!
I do not think, with this exposure,
we are going to find a soldier."

But then they found
some footprints
made by army boots.
They followed them
through the trees,
looking for recruits.
The trail led them

        through the woods,
            and through the woods,
                and through the woods,
              and then, what a surprise!
        they found before their eyes
nine army huts, all in a row,
their roofs, to the top almost, buried in snow.
Peter asked the soldiers
to come and join his ranks,
but they replied, regretfully,
"Thank you, but no thanks!"
The soldiers said "We're sorry
to hear your tale of woe,
bur it's much too cold for us to fight.
Please close the door and go."
 The Princess said "We've tried the north
The south, the east, the west.
Let's put our thinking caps on
and see what would be best."

7. To make a Paper Sailboat

Take a sheet of paper, and

1. Fold it in half.

2. Fold a corner to one inch from the cut edge.

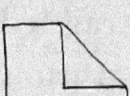

3. Do the same with the other corner.
   (there will be some overlap)

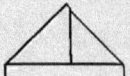

4. Fold the top one-inch edge strip back over the "sail".

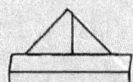

5. Fold the corners of that edge strip back over the "sail".

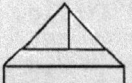

6. Turn it over and repeat 4 and 5 for the other edge strip.

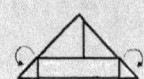

7. From below, spread the "sail" with your thumbs.

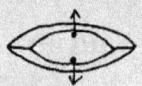

8. Fold the double-thickness of the one-inch strips back over the "sail" working all the way round its perimeter, and press it flat.

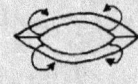

9. Spread your sails a little,
and you will be able to float your boat.

They put their thinking caps on
and learned "to help us most
we need to make a sail boat
and sail back to our coast."
That thought cheered them up a bit,
comforting their angst,
so they made themselves a sail boat
and took it to Murmansk.

(Tomorrow you can make
a sail boat of your own,
one just like the sailboat
they made to take them home.)

They took it to the sea shore
and put it in the sea.
They sailed away, back to their beach,
 and it was time for tea.

They walked across the sandy beach,
and crossed the grass, until
they reached the road,
    the road that winds
        round-and-round the hill.
So they all go
    round-and-round,
        until they reach the top,
          and at the top
            they stop.
They arrive at the door of the castle.
The door is very big.
It has a big knocker.
Peter reaches up for it and knocks at the door.
A voice from the Inner Guard says
"Halt! Who comes here?"
"We are Peter and Roger.
We are with the Princess and her cat.
We are here to have tea."
The Inner Guard says
"Halt, while I make due report."
The Inner Guard calls the Royal Equerry
"Honored Sir, outside the door of the castle
stand Peter and Roger
who are with the Princess and her cat.

They are here to have tea."
The Royal Equerry says
"You will admit them
with Grand Honors Nine Times."
.

The great big door opens wide. The Royal
Equerry bows and says "Welcome Home Your
Majesty." and to the Trumpeters he commands:
"Trumpeters! Grand Honors! Nine Times!"
The Royal Trumpeters raise their trumpets.
They trumpet "Rooty-Toot-Toot Nine Times"
    —such a wonderful din!
and the Princess and her friends walk in.

31

For tea they have hot-buttered crumpets,
and sardine sandwiches with their crusts cut off,
and chocolate cake, with jam in the middle
and white stuff on top,
and cat food for Sammi,
and dog food for Roger.
Then they put their thinking caps on.
They found "To save the Throne
what we really need are
some armies of our own."
Peter says "We will need our own armies.
We cannot call them a Red Army.
That belongs to the Red King.
We cannot call them a Black Army.
That belongs to the Black King.
We cannot call them a White Army.
That belongs to the White King.
What shall we call them?"
The Princess said "Let us call them
our Orange, Green, and Purple Armies."
"We'll need to have some banners:" said Sammi
"so we'll know which are our people."
so they made themselves some banners
that were orange, green, and purple.

(Tomorrow you can make some banners
so you can march around the house with them,
singing Rooty-Toot-Toot!)
but tomorrow is going to be a big day,
so today we need some sleep.

8. To make a Banner

You will need:

1. A broom stick.
2. An 18" piece of cane.
3. A page of a newspaper
4. A 4-foot piece of string
5. Scissors and a glue-stick.
   Here's what to do:

1. Tie the middle of the piece of string to the top of the broom stick.

2. Trim the newspaper so it is a couple of inches narrower than the cane. Fold it over the cane and glue parts of it together to stop it unfolding or sliding off.

3. Tie the strings to the ends of the cane. Lift high your banner as you march round the house singing Rooty-toot-toot!

Early next day the Red King arrives
at the head of his Red Army.
The Black King arrives
at the head of his Black Army.
The White King arrives
at the head of his White Army.
The Red King yells "Surrender!
      We are far more than you!"
Peter shouts "I don't think so.
      You're outnumbered one-to-two.
We have six armies here,
      and you have only three.
We have the Orange, Green and Purple,
the Pink, the Beige, the Blue;
and the Greys and Mauves are coming,
so we're not afraid of you."

There is a rumbling sound as the great door of the
castle opens with a thump, and out comes a
Royal Herald holding an Orange Banner. He is
followed by Peter waving his sword. Peter leads
a procession of people from the castle.
They hold pan lids from the kitchen and wave
bread knives in the air.

(from the bottom of the hill it looks like they are holding shields and waving swords.)
From the bottom of the hill it looks like they are an Orange Army.
They march around the castle,
    left, right, left, right,
and when they are round the back
    and out of sight
they duck back into the castle through the back door.
Once they are inside the castle they put on green hats. They lay down their pan lids and bread knives and pick up bows and arrows. (Tomorrow you can make a toy bow and arrow.)
The Herald puts down his orange banner and picks up a green banner. He joins the end of the Orange Army. Princess Maent follows him. She is wearing a green sash, and she carries a bow and arrow. She leads the people who are now wearing green hats, so it looks like the Orange Army is being followed by a Green Army.

9. To make a Toy Bow and Arrow

You will need:

1. A piece of cane almost as long as you are.
2. Some pieces half that length for arrows
3. String, construction paper, and cotton balls,
4. Scotch tape, masking tape, scissors and glue.

Here's what to do:

1. Wrap several turns of masking tape around the long cane about an inch from the each end (to stop the string from slipping.) Beyond the tape put a dab of glue on the cane.

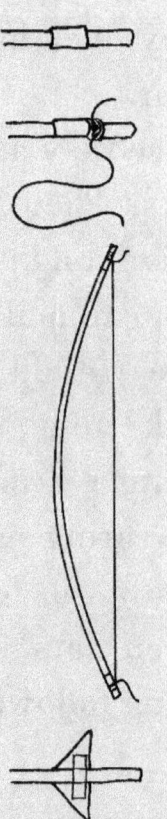

2. Tie a piece of string round the cane just outside of the tape, make a few turns round the cane and tie off again,

3. Bend the bow slightly and repeat at the other end, and you have a bow. This bow shoots gently, but be careful never to aim it at another person.

4. For the arrow flight cut a 2-inch square of paper diagonally in half. Set an arrow cane on it with an inch of the end extending. Put a 2 inch piece of scotch tape on the cane, press it all the way round the cane, and press the ends against the paper. For a soft landing glue a cotton ball to the other end.

When they are all outside the castle the Princess lifts her bow and shoots an arrow into the air. They all pick up their bows and arrows and shoot their arrows into the air, a great cloud of arrows.

They march around the castle and when they are out of sight they duck back into the castle through the back door.

Once they are inside the castle they take off their green hats and put on purple scarves. They lay down their bows and arrows and pick up baking pans and wooden spoons from the kitchen. The Royal Herald puts down his green banner and picks up a purple banner. He follows the Green Army so it looks like a Purple Army is following the Green Army.

The Royal Trumpeters follow the Royal Herald.

Rooty-toot-toot, toot-toot, toot-toot,

rooty,

tooty,

toot-toot!

They make a big noise, and the procession that follows them makes an even bigger noise as they bang on their pans with their wooden spoons.

(Tomorrow, if you have a friend you can play with, your friend can bang on a pan with a wooden spoon while you lead the way with your banner, both of you singing rooty-toot-toot.)

Roger and Sammi are way up high.

They are on the castle roof.

Sammi is draped in a pink blanket.

She is wearing her golden crown.

She is sitting on Roger's back.

From below it looks like Sammi is the Pink Queen,

sitting on her black horse,

and waiting for her Pink Army to arrive.

The Black King
     and the White King
         march up to the Red King.
The Black King says
"This isn't what we signed-up-for.
We've three armies, but they have more!"
The White King says
"Things are getting out of hand.
Look, they've even got a band!"
The Black King says
"In this sudden circumstance
I don't think we would stand a chance."
The White King says
"We're outnumbered with our three
so we are going home for tea."

When the Red King saw
his troops retreat
he got so mad
he stamped his feet.
He stamped his feet
And stubbed his toe
and that just made
his anger grow.
He was itching for a fight.
The words he used were not polite.
He ended up in such a rage
I think we'd better turn the page.

The Princess said "That's it! No more!
  I think we've had enough of war!
This is where the fighting ends:
  tomorrow we will all be friends.
I don't want neighbors in a stew.
  I think we'll let them play here too."
Meanwhile, the people were so pleased by the way things worked out they made Peter a prince and from that point on he was to be called
  "His Royal Highness the Prince Peter."
Prince Peter lived in the castle with
  "Her Magnificence the Princess Maent"
and tomorrow you can start to build
a model of their castle.
  Sammi said "I'm glad that's over!
Now things can get back to normal."
  Roger agreed.
He said
  "Rowf!"

Now you can build a model of the Castle,

and when you're done, for instant fame,
you could send photos of your creations to
<u>princess.maent@gmail.com</u>
to be featured on the official Princess Maent
⊙ Instagram account: @Princess.Maent

To build your model you will need. . .

1. Construction paper, five sheets, 8½x11 or 9x12:
   a sheet of yellow (for the sandy beach)
   a sheet of dark blue (for the sea)
   a sheet of light grey (for the Castle), and
   2 sheets of green (for the Hill)

2. White chalk, or white paint and a small brush.

3. Two pieces of cardboard, one 2¼ inches square and one 12 inches square.

4. A "small" (8 oz.) coffee cup from a local coffee shop. It should be about 4 inches high and 3½ wide at the rim..

5. Pencil, ruler, scissors, white glue, a glue-stick, scotch tape, a pointy toothpick and a large pin.

To make the base for the model

1. Glue the blue sheet of construction paper to the 12" square of cardboard so its edge lines up with the edge of the cardboard.

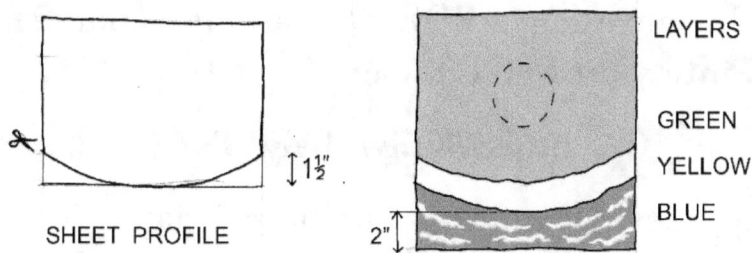

SHEET PROFILE   1½"   2"   LAYERS

GREEN
YELLOW
BLUE

2. Trim the long edge off a sheet of yellow paper and a sheet of green paper. Start 1½ inches from the corner and cut in a curve that meets the edge of the paper in the middle, and curves back to match the first cut. It's OK if it wiggles a bit.

3. Glue the yellow sheet on top of the blue sheet, keeping it a bit back so we see about 2 inches of blue at the middle.

4. Glue the green sheet on top of the yellow sheet so its uncut edge lines up with the back edge of the cardboard.

5. Make white wiggly chalk or paint lines on the blue sheet to look like ocean waves.

To build your model . . .

The parts you will need to cut out to build your model are illustrated on the following two pages. You can download and print these pages by downloading a PDF file here by typing this link into your web browser:

https://bit.ly/2BelyVP

Print these downloads on colored paper if you have it: green for the Hill sheet and grey for the Castle sheet.

If you prefer to scan the illustrations in the book you should, in the "Preview" mode, set the boundaries of your image so they crop off the grey borders; then print the scans "fit-to-page" on "8½ x 11-portrait" colored papers.

If you prefer to use a photocopier (or a print shop) you should make a photocopy of each page, then with scissors trim off the grey borders, set the zoom control of the machine to 200%, load the machine with colored papers, and print.

Note: You may have to trim the width of your colored papers to 8½ inches to run them in the machine—that's OK.

The Hill Sheet

Print a 200% blow-up of this sheet on 8½x11 green paper.

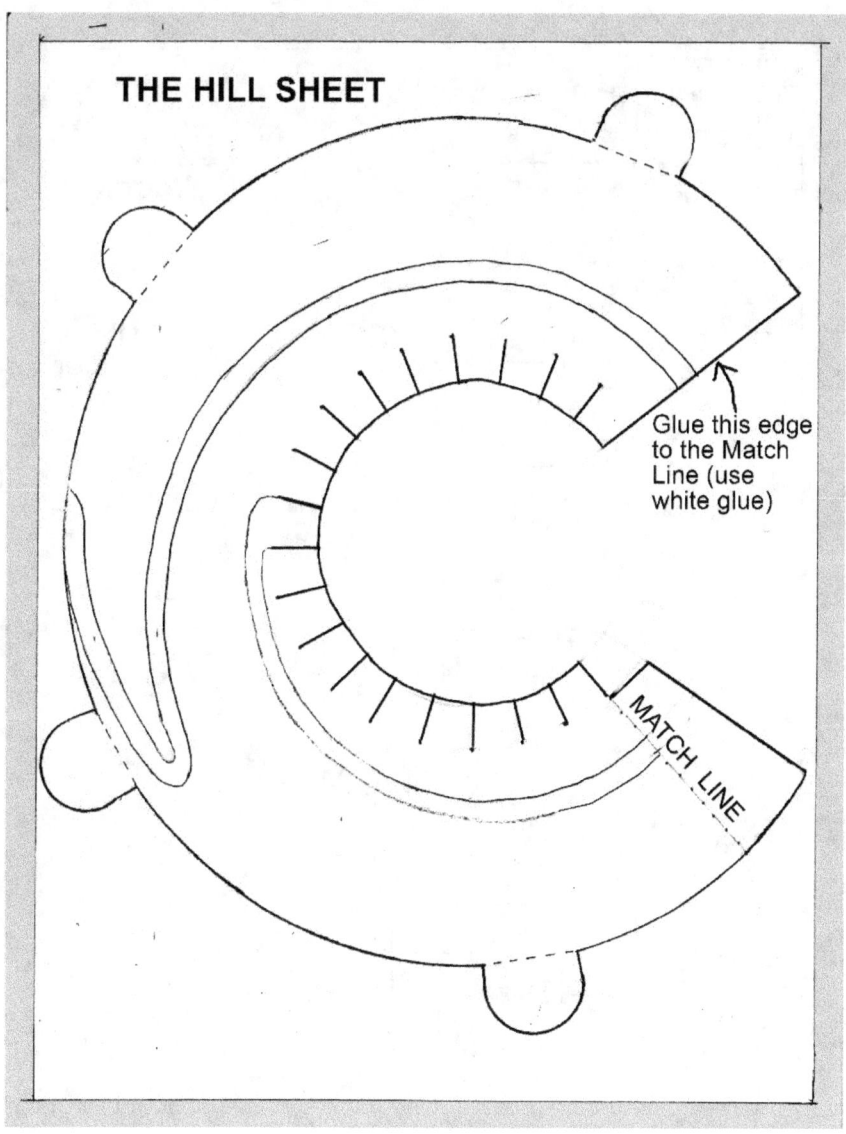

The Castle Sheet

Print a 200% blow-up of this sheet on 8½x11 gray paper.

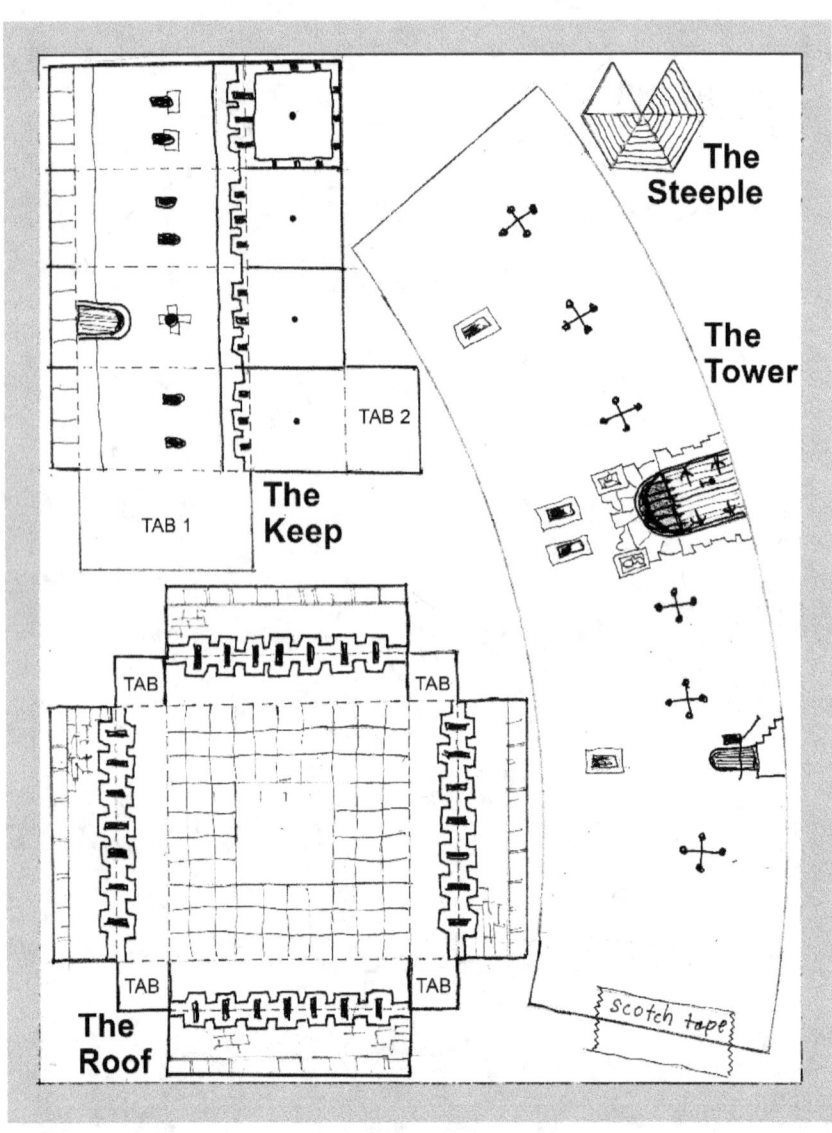

To build the Hill

1. Apply white glue to the rim of the coffee cup and glue it to the middle of the green sheet on the base.

2. Cut out the shape on the "Hill" sheet, including the slots between the tabs that surround the central hole.

3. Chalk or paint the curving lines that make a "winding path". It's OK to be messy.

4. Bend the cut-out so its end covers the "match line" to make a cone, glue it down, and let it dry.

5. Apply glue to the underside of the four tabs at the edge of the shape and to the underside of the central tabs. Push the cone down over the coffee cup keeping the join to the rear. Press the outer tabs to the base and the inner tabs to the coffee cup. If the Hill will not reach the ground, cut the central slots a bit deeper.

To build the Tower

1. Cut out the tower shape.

2. With a small piece of scotch tape attach the flap to the coffee cup and wrap it round, covering the tabs, positioning it so the castle door faces the ocean.

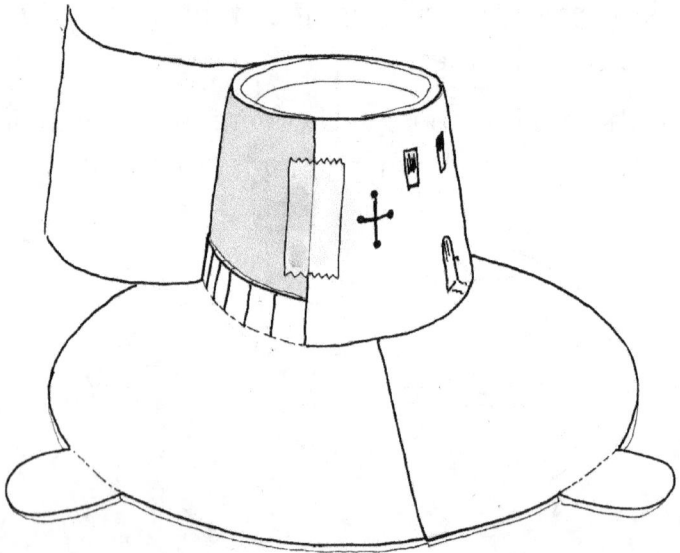

3. When you are satisfied with its position apply a thin film of whit glue to the underside of the sheet and wrap it around the cup. Trim off any excess paper.

4. Glue the small 2¼ inches square of cardboard to the top of the coffee cup and allow it to dry.

To make the Roof

1. Cut out the roof shape, including the four small cuts to separate the tabs in the corners. Make creases on all the fold lines then flatten out the sheet.

2. Make fold No. 1 (a fold-over on to itself) and glue-stick the back so the wall pattern is visible on both sides of the wall. Repeat for the opposite side.

3. Fold up fold No. 2 on both sides, then fold up No 3.

4. Fold up the tabs (Fold No. 4) and glue them to the outside of the other wall sections.

5. Fold over Fold No. 5 and glue down to cover the tabs.

6. Glue the complete roof to the cardboard square on the top of the tower.

Folds for the Roof

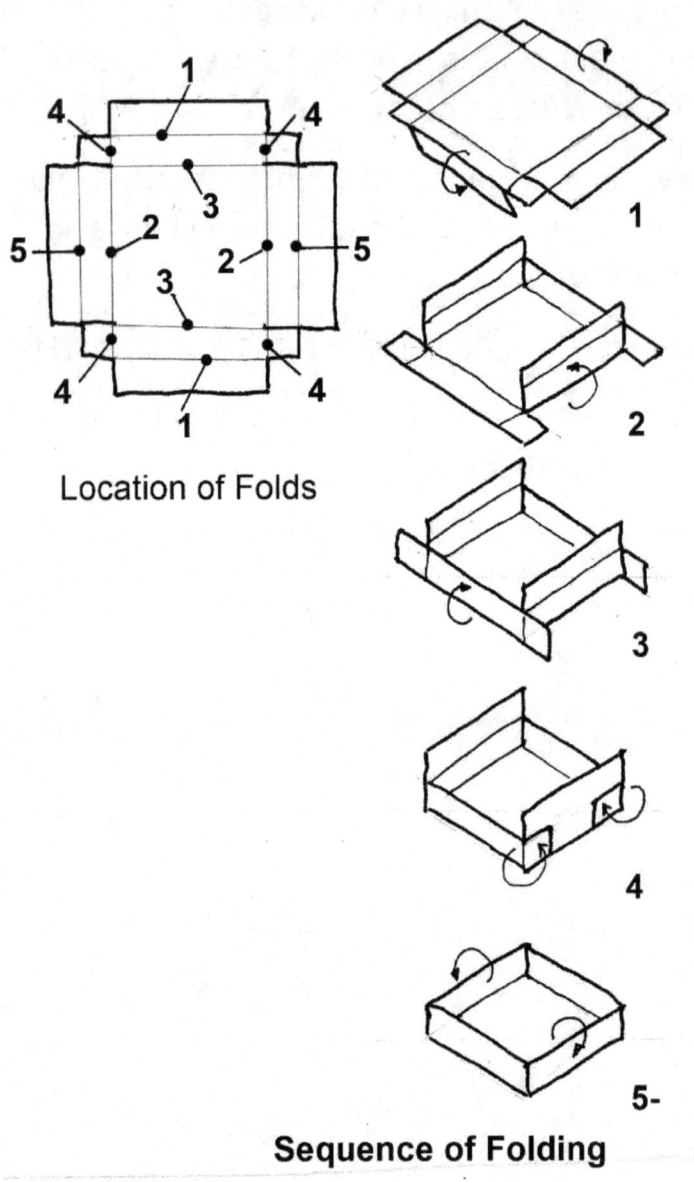

Location of Folds

Sequence of Folding

To build the Keep

(that's the smaller central Tower
—a safe refuge if the Castle is attacked,)

1. Cut out the Keep shape. Make a hole that is big enough for the toothpick to pass through in the middle of each square panel.

2. Make the four long corner folds, and glue the side flap to the inside of the first side to make a square tube. Glue the top flap to the opposite side. When the glue is dry glue down the other three flaps..

3. Poke the toothpick up through the holes from the inside until one inch protrudes. Put a dab of white glue on the join and let it dry.

4. Cut out the steeple, fold all four corners, and glue the last tiled section over the plain one.

5. Push the steeple over the toothpick (now a flag pole) until one inch is exposed. Put some glue on the other end and push it through the hole in the keep. Add a tiny triangular flag.

6. Fold out the four flaps at the bottom of the keep and glue them to the tower roof.

Assembling the Keep

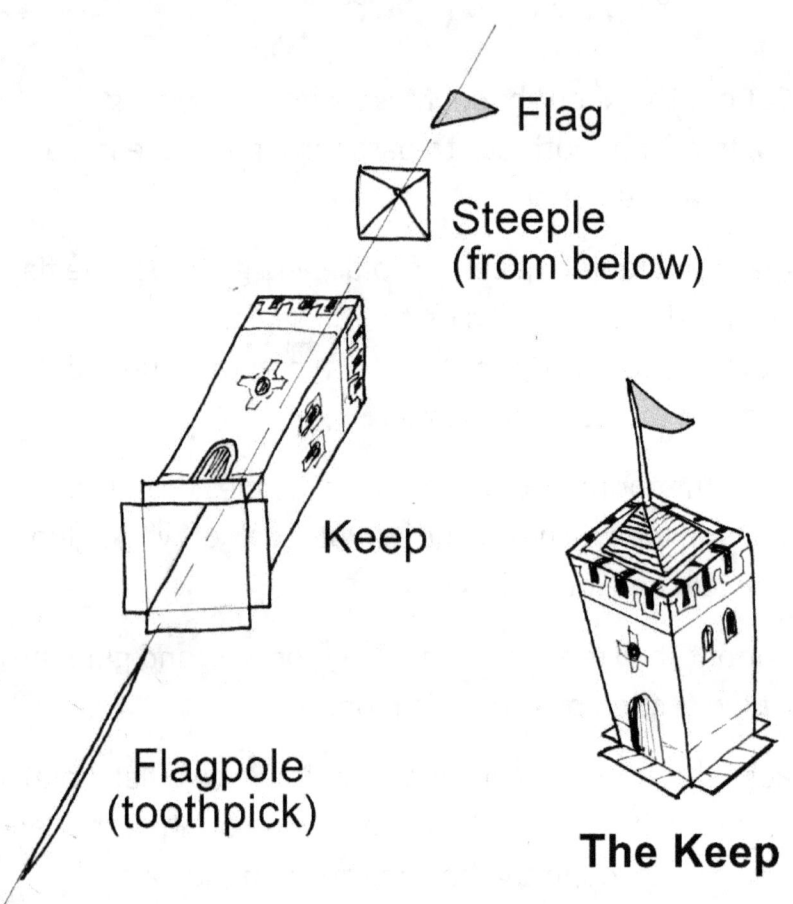

Flag

Steeple
(from below)

Keep

Flagpole
(toothpick)

The Keep

If you are feeling a bit more ambitious . . .

you could build your castle on a rocky promontory as seen on the front cover of this book (instead of on a green hill as illustrated on the back cover.) To do this you will need a piece of cardboard, a 12 inches square piece of brown wrapping paper, and an additional coffee cup.

1. Cut out a 3½ inch diameter circle from your piece of cardboard (you could trace around the rim of a coffee cup.)

2. Glue an upside-down coffee cup to the model base as before, then glue the cardboard disc to the cup's bottom.

3. Crumple up the paper into a ball (that's the fun part) then flatten it out and glue it's central area to the disk.

4. Press the paper towards the coffee cup, but not so strongly as to flatten out all the bumps (so it will still have a rocky look.) Trim off excess paper where it meets the ground and use a few dabs of glue to hold it in place. Voila!

5. Wrap the "Tower" wall round the other coffee-cup base as before, trim off the rest of the cup and glue to the rock.

If your rocky pinnacle rose out of a sea of blue paper instead of being land-locked you would have to build a bridge to connect your castle to the shore. You could be the first to demonstrate this on Instagram!

Decorating your Model with Trees

Your model will be more realistic if you plant some trees around it. For these you can use the tops of almost any plant such as Tansy or Joe Pye Weed that has small leaves or florets. You could gather some from a hedgerow or anywhere where there are some weeds, but use just one sort for your model, and snip the stems so your trees are less than 2 inches high, so the Castle will tower above them.

Tansy   *Joe Pye Weed*   *Yew*   *Cedar*

Your trees will look best if you plant them in clumps. Make holes in your model base, put in a dab of glue, and press in your tree trunk.

A Sailboat for your Model

Here is a design for a small sailboat that you can set in the ocean. You will need:

1. Two pieces of white paper: one piece 1½ x ½ inch, and the other piece 1 inch square.

2. a wood toothpick, scissors and white glue.

To build your model

1. Fold down the corners of the oblong strip of paper as shown in the diagram. Make a hole in it for the toothpick.

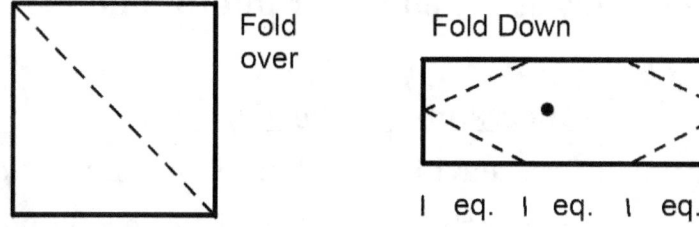

Fold over

Fold Down

I eq. I eq. I eq. I

2. Cut your toothpick to 1½ inches long.

3. Fold the square paper in half diagonally. Put some white glue on the toothpick and press two of the short sides against it. Let it dry.

4. Push the blunt end of the toothpick through the hole you made in the bottom of your boat.

5. Make a hole in the ocean on your model base, put some glue in it, push the blunt end of the toothpick into the hole, and press the bottom of the boat to touch the ocean..

The adventure continues!

Continue to adventure by following
@Princess.Maent on ⦾ Instagram.

and don't forget to send your photos and
comments to
<u>princess.maent@gmail.com</u>
to have your creations featured on the official
Instagram account! . . . and that is where you can
see what others are doing too.

www.ingramcontent.com/pod-product-compliance
Lightning Source LLC
Chambersburg PA
CBHW071348130626
46556CB00005B/2088